Forest Fire

BY

Ed Hanson

THE BARCLAY FAMILY ADVENTURES

Development and Production: Laurel Associates, Inc.
Cover and Interior Art: Black Eagle Productions

SADDLEBACK
PUBLISHING·INC.
Three Watson
Irvine, CA 92618-2767

Website: www.sdlback.com

ISBN 1-56254-553-1

Printed in the United States of America
08 07 06 05   9 8 7 6 5 4 3 2 1

CONTENTS

MEET THE BARCLAYS

Paul Barclay
A fun-loving father of three who takes his kids on his travels whenever he can.

Ann Barclay
The devoted mother who manages the homefront during Paul's many absences as an on-site construction engineer.

Jim Barclay
The eldest child, Jim is a talented athlete with his eye on a football scholarship at a major college.

Aaron Barclay
Three years younger than Jim, he's inquisitive, daring, and an absolute whiz in science class.

Pam Barclay
Adopted from Korea as a baby, Pam is a spunky middle-schooler who more than holds her own with her lively older brothers.

CHAPTER 1

Arriving in Montana

Aaron and Jim were in the garage pulling their fishing gear together. Tomorrow they would be flying to Montana for a vacation with their father. He had planned five days of hiking, camping, and trout fishing in the mountains.

"Montana has some of the best trout fishing in the lower 48 states," Paul Barclay had said. "It's a real thrill to catch plump native trout on a light fly rod! And fried over a campfire—they'll melt in your mouth!"

Aaron had a pencil and pad of paper. He listed each item as Jim packed it.

"Two Fenwick rods," Jim said. "Also two reels with line. I've got my fishing vest, Aaron, but I can't find yours."

An hour later, the boys had all their gear packed. Aaron had made a list of all the items they still needed to buy.

The next morning their father arrived right on time. Their mother, Ann, and their little sister, Pam, helped the boys pack the gear into the car.

As they pulled out of the driveway, Ann called out, "Have a great time, guys! Bring us back some fish!"

"We will," the boys yelled back. "Love you, Mom!"

An hour later, the three Barclays boarded a Northwest Airlines plane and settled in for a four-hour flight.

Aaron asked his father about bears.

"I sure hope we see some," he said.

"Well, there *are* bears in Montana, Aaron—both grizzlies and black bears. So, we might see some," Paul answered.

"What about elk?" Jim asked.

"There are lots of elk in Montana. We definitely should see some."

"And deer?" Aaron added.

"Yes, deer, too. But they'll probably be mule deer—not white-tails like we have in the east."

"Mule deer are larger, aren't they, Dad?" Jim asked.

"Yes, they are. And, by the way, did you guys remember to bring cameras?"

Both boys looked at each other. "Oops—that's one thing we forgot."

"No problem," Paul said. "We'll pick up a couple of those disposable cameras. They aren't too expensive and they take pretty good pictures."

Finally, the airliner circled the city of Bozeman in preparation for landing. The plane touched the ground with a slight bounce and taxied to the gate. The airport was surprisingly crowded.

"Thousands of hunters travel to Montana every fall," Paul explained. "Most are after elk, but some come for the moose and deer."

After picking up their baggage and renting a car, Paul stopped at the nearest supermarket.

"We'll get our supplies for the trip here," Paul said. "Jim, go over to the drugstore and pick up two disposable cameras. Aaron and I will meet you at the checkout counter."

Aaron pushed the cart while Paul loaded it up. When his father wasn't looking, Aaron dropped some of his favorite goodies into the cart.

Paul raised his eyebrows when the groceries were being rung up. "Where did all this junk food come from?" he asked.

Then he smiled at Aaron and playfully punched his arm. "It's okay, son," he said. "But remember—*you* have to carry it."

They paid the bill, loaded the car, and headed out of Bozeman toward the Gallatin Canyon.

CHAPTER 2

Buying Supplies

It was a beautiful autumn day. The air was brisk, and bright sunlight glistened off the mountains on both sides of the road.

Jim and Aaron were excited. What could be better than camping in the wilds of Montana? They could hardly wait to see the wild animals—especially bears—and catch their first native trout.

The Gallatin River ran alongside the road. As they entered Gallatin Canyon, Paul noticed right away that the water level in the river was very low.

"There's been no rain here for weeks," he said. "We'll have to be very careful with our campfires. Look how dry everything is!"

As they continued up the canyon, the road crossed and recrossed the river.

Finally, Paul slowed down. He turned the car into the driveway of Elmer's Motel and Restaurant. The Barclays tumbled out of the car and looked around them.

A tall man about the same age as the boys' grandfather was at the door to greet them. It was Elmer himself, the owner. He wore a western-style shirt, jeans, and cowboy boots.

"Welcome to Elmer's!" he said with a smile.

Paul introduced himself, Jim, and Aaron. After they all shook hands, Paul signed the motel guest book.

"Is this the first trip to Montana for you boys?" Elmer asked.

Aaron was quick to answer. "Yes, sir. We're anxious to see some wildlife— especially grizzly bears!"

"Is that so? Well, if you boys are interested in grizzlies, I know somebody you should talk to. But, why don't we take your things to your room first?"

After getting settled in their room, the next stop was Elmer's restaurant. It had been a long day, and they were all hungry. They met Elmer's wife, Helen, at the restaurant. She showed them where to sit and took their order.

"We're starving! Buffalo burgers all around," Paul said.

"And French fries," Jim added.

"And pickles!" Aaron chimed in.

"You've got it. Buffalo burgers it is," Helen laughed.

When they'd eaten the delicious burgers, Elmer came over to their table. This time he was wearing a cowboy hat. He sat down next to Jim.

"If you want to know about grizzly bears," he said, "you should talk to Zeb Parker. He knows every inch of these mountains from the Gallatin Canyon to Yellowstone—and that covers more than 50 miles. Zeb has had a good many encounters with bears. In fact, eight years ago he lost part of his leg to a grizzly."

Aaron's mouth dropped open. His eyes were wide.

"We'd sure like to meet Mr. Parker. Where can we find him?" Paul asked.

"Well, aren't you lucky?" Elmer chuckled. "Here he is, coming through the door right now."

CHAPTER 3

Zeb Parker

Turning around, the Barclays saw a lean and weathered man walk in and take a table. He was a thin fellow, but he looked muscular and strong. He wore old clothes and walked with a limp.

The boys and their dad walked over to the man's table.

"Excuse me, are you Zeb Parker?" Paul asked politely.

"Yeah. Why do you want to know?" Zeb looked hard at Paul and the boys.

"Well, Mr. Parker, my sons and I are going camping in the mountains. We hear that no one can give us more information about bears than you can."

"That's probably so," the man said in a raspy, low voice, "and you fellas might as well call me Zeb—everybody does."

"Okay, Zeb, I'd be happy to buy you drinks and dinner if you'd share some of your experiences with us."

That seemed to spark Zeb's interest.

"For a free dinner and drinks, I'd talk to the devil. Sit down," he said, pointing to the other chairs at his table.

Zeb started telling Paul and the boys all about grizzlies. He talked about their size and strength.

"And they're really fast," Zeb told them. "No one can outrun a grizzly."

Once Zeb got talking, it was hard to get him to stop. He went on and on about grizzly bears. He told of their huge size, their long, knife-sharp claws, and their fearlessness.

"One thousand pounds of pure fury—that's what a grizzly is."

Finally, Jim asked, "What happened to your leg, Mr. Parker?"

For a moment, Zeb stopped talking. He glared at Jim. *That's the end of this conversation,* Paul thought to himself. But then Zeb broke into a grin.

"You know, son, you're the first person with the guts to ask me that," he said. "Everyone else just stares and backs away. Okay, then—I'll tell you what happened.

"It was about eight years ago. I was alone in the mountains, marking trails for tenderfoots that I'd be guiding on a hiking trip. I guess I just got too busy thinking about what I was doing to stay alert. Then, when I rounded a bend, I suddenly came face to face with a sow and two cubs!

"Well, that mother bear took one look at me and charged. There was no tree in sight, so I did the next best thing. I rolled up in a ball on the ground."

Aaron could just picture Zeb curled up into a human ball!

"That big bear toyed with me for an hour," Zeb continued. "Finally, out of boredom, I guess, she swiped at me with her paw and left. But she had taken almost three pounds of flesh off my leg with that one swipe!

"I tied a kerchief around my leg to stop the bleeding. Then I had to crawl nearly four miles to reach the road. To this day, I don't blame that bear. She was only trying to protect her cubs."

Pausing, Zeb took his pipe from his pocket. As he lit up, a circle of white smoke curled above his head.

Then Zeb looked right at Jim. "Some people say the great white shark is the greatest killing machine in the ocean. Well, that may be. But I know for sure that the grizzly bear is the greatest killing machine on land. You can bet on that!

"One time I saw a grizzly square off against a big bull elk. For a while, the elk did a pretty good job of holding that bear off with its giant antlers. Those sharp points can be quite a weapon, you know.

"But the elk made one mistake. And

in an eyeblink, that bear was ripping at its neck. I can still hear the dying groans of that poor animal. That elk had to weigh at least 700 pounds—but the bear dragged it into the woods like it was a little rag doll."

Finally, Paul said, "Thanks so much, Zeb. You've given us a lot of valuable information. But I have just one last question. What's the best way to avoid meeting up with a bear?"

"Make a lot of noise," Zeb said. "But if you do meet up with one, pepper spray works pretty well."

Paul paid Zeb's bill and they said goodbye. Outside the restaurant, Aaron finally spoke up.

"You know what? I hope I *never* see a grizzly bear," he said.

Jim and Paul laughed.

CHAPTER 4

Getting Ready

The huge grizzly stared down the trail at the approaching hikers. The bear was well-hidden in the thick underbrush. The hikers had no idea it was there. But it could see them!

Hot saliva dripped from the grizzly's upper teeth. Its black eyes glared at the intruders. After all, this mountain was *his*—people had no business here. As the huge animal stretched its front legs, it bared four inches of sharp claws. The hikers were 75 yards away now.

Soon the bear would charge from its hiding place. The hikers would panic and run. Maybe one of them would make it to a tree and get away. But the bear was sure to catch up with one or two of them. He *knew* he would.

At 25 yards, the grizzly burst out of the thicket. The three startled hikers screamed and ran. The smallest of them stumbled and fell. He stared into the bear's mouth. . . .

"Aaahh!" Aaron screamed as he bolted upright in bed. His body was shaking and wet with perspiration.

"What are you yelling about?" Jim called from the bed across the room.

"Oh, Jim!" Aaron said in a shaky voice. "I just had the worst dream! A great big bear was attacking me."

Jim yawned loudly. "Go back to sleep, Aaron. There aren't any bears here," he said as he dozed off.

The next morning Paul and the boys enjoyed a hearty breakfast. Helen served them big plates of bacon, eggs, toast, and tall glasses of orange juice.

While they ate, Aaron told his father about his dream.

"Don't worry, son," Paul said. "I

promise I won't let any bears catch you. I think you're letting Zeb Parker's stories get to you."

"I guess you're right, Dad. But I'd rather not see any bears on this trip."

"Have a wonderful time," Helen called out as they were leaving. "Catch lots of trout, and remember to be careful with your campfires. The woods are very dry right now."

"Our next stop is the bait shop," Paul said. "We need fishing licenses, flies, and some fish line. Then we're off to the woods, boys!"

The Barclays loaded their packs and camping gear into the car. In a few minutes, Paul pulled up into a parking lot in front of a small building.

"Come on in with me," he said.

Several boxes of fishing lures and flies sat on the counter. Bins of reels and line flanked the aisles. Big maps on the walls showed all the lakes and streams in the area.

"Hi," said a young woman behind the counter. According to her nametag, this was Tory, a fishing guide. "You fellows going fishing today?"

"We sure are," Paul said. "My sons and I are going to Lodge Pole Lake. We plan to stay there for six days."

"I took some folks up there just last week," Tory said. "We hiked in one day and fished the second day. The third day we hiked out."

Tory helped them choose the flies they'd need.

"I think you're going to need some hoppers, too," she suggested. "Why don't you try this one? Joe's hopper is made of plastic. It looks something like a grasshopper. I think you'll have good luck with it this time of year."

When they'd made their choices, she put the flies and hoppers into a bag.

"Just be really careful with your cookstove," she reminded them. "The forest is very dry these days. Any little spark could start a big forest fire."

"Uh—Tory. Did you see any bears last week?" Aaron asked.

"Yes, we saw three black bears. One of them was cinnamon color. But we didn't see any brown bears," she said.

Aaron and Jim looked confused. How could a black bear be the color of cinnamon?

Tory went on to explain. "Brown bears *are* grizzly bears. Grizzlies have small ears and a hump on their backs. And they often have silver fur around their necks. They can be real big.

"Black bears are much smaller," she continued. "They have larger ears and shorter claws than grizzly bears. And they *do* come in all different colors—so I say a black bear is cinnamon color if it's reddish-brown.

"Do you know why brown bears can't climb trees? Because their claws are too long. If you see a brown bear, get up a tree—if there's a tree around, that is."

Aaron listened intently. He hoped he could remember all of that.

"All kinds of bears can be dangerous, of course. But grizzlies are the most dangerous," Tory continued. "Just to be on the safe side, why don't you take a can of pepper spray?"

She handed them a large can.

"You can fasten it to your belt. Then it's always ready," she said. "Notice this little orange clip? It keeps you from pushing down the trigger. If a bear charges you, pull out the orange clip. Wait until the animal is about 10 yards away, and then aim for its face. The sting of the spray will make him run away.

"Here's a card with drawings of animal tracks. Look—here's what a bear footprint looks like. This card will help you read the animal prints you see on the trail."

Paul paid for the fishing supplies. Then he took the pepper spray and hooked it onto his belt.

Then Paul and his sons piled into the car. They didn't say much as they drove up the canyon toward Lodge Pole Lake.

CHAPTER 5

Hiking to Lodge Pole Lake

The ride was hot and dusty. When they finally arrived at the trailhead, the boys were glad to get out of the car.

They spread the gear on the ground and divided it up. Paul carried most of it, and the two boys divided up the rest. Paul made sure that Aaron carried all the junk food.

A sign at the trailhead said:

GRIZZLY BEAR HABITAT
USE CAUTION

Jim made a mental note to look for trees that would do for a quick getaway.

The three Barclays started up the trail.

Clouds of dirt puffed up around them at every step. They noticed that heavy dust coated the plants along the trail.

They climbed up and up and up. As they made their way through open fields of sagebrush, they passed little streams with green plants growing alongside.

They climbed through forests of large evergreens. In the distance they saw even more mountains.

Soon Paul and Aaron were growing tired—but not Jim. After working out for football, he was in good shape. While they stopped in the shade for a short rest, Paul studied the map.

"We don't have far to go now," he said. "And soon the climb will be much easier."

After climbing for another half-hour, the trail became less steep. They took the time to look around and enjoy the scenery. The day was getting warmer, and there wasn't a cloud in the sky.

Their next stop was near a stream.

There they ate some breakfast bars and trail mix. For a cold drink, they filtered water from the rushing stream.

Aaron wandered up the stream. He noticed some footprints in the mud and stopped to examine them. It looked like a big man had walked barefoot through the mud—except that the toe was on the *outside* of the foot.

"Hey, Dad! Jim!" Aaron called out. "Come see what I found!"

Paul and Jim walked over to him and looked at the footprints. Jim got out the track card.

"I think a bear made that track, Aaron," Jim said. "Look at this card. A bear has his big toe on the outside."

"Look for the claw marks," Paul said. "If they're close to the toe, it's a black bear. If the claw marks are farther away, it's a grizzly bear."

Aaron studied the card carefully. "Black bear," he said.

"Good," Paul said. "You're learning

to read prints. Okay, then. Is everybody ready to push on? I think we can be at the lake in about three hours."

"Yes," the boys said in one voice.

They were eager to get to the lake. For one thing, they wanted to get the heavy packs off their backs. But most of all, they looked forward to setting up camp and then doing some fishing.

CHAPTER 6

Setting Up Camp

About 5 o'clock that afternoon, the Barclays reached the lake.

Jim and Aaron ran to the water and took off their boots. Wading barefoot, they washed the dust from their faces and arms. They splashed each other. The cool water felt good.

"Let's set up camp now," Paul said. "The kitchen is first. It should be near the spring, but not *too* near. We have to keep the spring clean, because that's where we get our drinking water.

"Our sleeping area needs to be away from the kitchen. That way, a bear looking for a midnight snack won't mistake us for marshmallows!"

He pointed at the sky. "And we need

29

a spot that gets the morning sun to dry up the dew. It should also be a high spot. Then, any rainwater will flow *away* from the tent—not that it's rained lately.

"We'll put up the tent away from any dead trees. A big wind could blow a dead tree down on us.

"And lastly, we need to pitch our tent in front of a tree. Then we'll have a tree to climb if a bear comes to visit."

Aaron listened closely. "Wow, Dad!" he laughed. "Camping in bear country means having to follow a whole lot of rules, doesn't it?"

"Oh, and there's one more rule—no food in the tent," Paul said. "All our food must be hoisted up a tree at night *and* during the day when we're fishing."

Paul and Aaron searched for a spot for the tent. They found a grassy knoll. There was a medium-size tree nearby, and the ground was high and flat.

"This will be fine," Paul said. "See, boys? The sun will shine in the tent door and wake us up in the morning."

Aaron and Paul put up the tent.

Jim found a spot near the spring for the kitchen. Several fallen trees there would make good seats. A large flat rock would serve as a table. Their cookstove would also fit on a nearby rock.

Jim got out a small folding shovel. He used it to scrape up leaves and branches from the campsite. Then, wanting to be careful of fire, he threw the brush far from the kitchen.

Jim wondered about hiding the food in a tree. Didn't Tory say that a black bear could climb a tree?

If the bear could climb the tree, he could get the food. He wondered just what his dad had in mind.

Jim got out the cooking pots and the tin plates and cups, while Aaron went to the spring for water. Then Jim unpacked some soup mix, rice, and dried fruit. They were all hungry and thirsty after the long hike. He made lemonade for everyone.

Paul and Aaron came wandering into the kitchen area.

"Thanks for the lemonade," Aaron said as he drained his cup. "What's for supper? I'm so hungry I feel like I could eat a bear."

Everyone laughed. "You'd better hope a hungry bear is nowhere near us. He might want to eat *you*," Jim teased.

After dinner, Jim boiled some water to wash and rinse the dishes. He scrubbed the pots. Then he threw the dishwater far away from the spring.

"Time to put the food up the tree," said Dad. "First, get it all in one big bag. Use one of those plastic garbage bags, boys. Then find a piece of rope.

"Now, let's go measure off a distance of 100 yards or so from the tent. Then look for a tree with a sturdy branch about 15 feet above the ground."

Paul pointed to a lodge pole pine. "That tree will do nicely. Tie a rock to one end of the rope. Then we'll throw the rock and the rope over the branch."

Jim followed his dad's directions. After missing on his first try, he finally threw the rock and rope over the tree limb. Then Paul showed him how to slide the rope toward the end of the limb.

"Now, tie the food bag to one end of the rope," Paul said. "Then pull on the other end so the food will be hoisted into the air—away from the tree trunk."

When the food was out of reach, Paul said, "Now all we need to do is anchor this end of the rope to a tree or a rock."

The boys were now very tired. They brushed their teeth and set their boots outside the tent. Then they unrolled their mats and sleeping bags and snuggled down. For the time being, they were too tired to think about bears.

Paul made one last check of the kitchen to make sure the fire was out. Then he crawled into his sleeping bag.

Peace at last! Then they suddenly

heard a loud howl coming from the other side of the lake. First one *AA-OOOH*, and then several loud *AA-OOH*s.

First Jim sat up. Then Aaron. Paul lay in his sleeping bag.

"It's just a pack of wolves, I'd guess. They won't bother us," Paul said.

The Barclays went to sleep.

CHAPTER 7

The First Trout

The next morning the sun woke the campers at 5:30. One by one, they crawled out of the tent and pulled on their boots.

"Not a cloud in the sky. What a day!" Aaron said cheerfully.

Paul suggested they go down to the lake and fish for an hour or two.

"The trout always bite better in the morning," he said. "Then we can come back and cook up some breakfast."

Paul got out the fishing rods. He tied flies on two of them and a hopper on the other.

"Who wants to fish with a hopper?" Paul asked.

"I'll try it," Aaron volunteered.

"Okay, son. Good luck."

Although Paul was the most experienced fly fisherman, Jim got the first strike. He'd cast his small brown fly about 25 yards from the shoreline. No sooner had it landed on the water than a large trout shot out of the water and grabbed it! It made a big splash as it fell back into the water.

The fish was heading for the middle of the lake! Jim's reel whined as the line unspooled. Just minutes later, Jim had worked the trout back near the shoreline.

"Remember to keep the tip of your rod up," Paul yelled.

The fish was tiring now. Holding his fishing rod out of the way, Jim lowered the net and scooped up the trout.

"Nicely done, Jimbo!" Paul said. The trout was 16 inches long. "That's a real beauty. A couple more like that and we have tonight's dinner."

They fished for another hour and caught several more trout. But as the sun rose higher and higher in the sky, the fish stopped biting.

"What do you say we go back and have a little breakfast?" Paul said.

Aaron suggested pancakes. Jim got the fire going while Paul lowered the food bag. He and Aaron got out pancake mix, maple syrup, instant orange juice, and coffee. In a few minutes, they were sitting around their stone table enjoying breakfast.

"Why is it that food usually tastes so much better when it's cooked outdoors?" Aaron asked.

"I don't know, son," Paul answered. "Maybe you're just hungrier."

After breakfast they all helped clean up. When the dishes were washed and the food was safely back in the tree, Jim and Aaron slipped into their swimsuits. The morning dew had burned off now, and the temperature was in the 80s.

Back at the lake, Jim and Aaron paddled around near the shoreline. Since both boys were excellent swimmers, Paul didn't worry about them in the water. After a while, they climbed up on a large boulder and stretched out. They dozed lazily as the sun dried them off.

Paul walked down to the lake to find his sons. "If you're finished swimming, what do you say we take a walk?"

"Sure, Dad," they answered.

After returning to the campsite to get their clothes, the boys joined their dad.

Suddenly, they saw a little brown animal peeking at them from behind a bush. When it ran around a rock, they could see its brown and white ears and beady black eyes. Including its long, black-tipped tail, the weasel was about a foot long.

Paul and the boys laughed as they watched it run up a tree, jump down, and scamper off through the grass.

"Okay, boys, which way do you want to hike?" Paul asked.

"Let's just follow the stream," Jim

said. "Along the way we can keep an eye out for trees to climb."

The stream led them up and around a hill. Within a few minutes, they came to a meadow where dried flowers blew in the wind. Clouds of dust puffed up as they walked along. Then suddenly, Paul stopped.

"Don't move," he whispered. "I see a bear up ahead."

Paul rested his hand on Aaron's shoulder and spoke in a low voice. "I can't tell yet what kind of bear it is. He has his head down—but I can see his color—he's brown."

Now Aaron and Jim could see the bear, too. "Maybe it won't see us. It's about 50 yards away," Jim whispered.

Paul lifted his head to test the air. "We're upwind of him, so I'm pretty sure that he can't smell us."

Jim nodded and looked around. "Look! There's a good climbing tree."

He pointed behind them to a big tree

that seemed to be about 20 yards away.

"Good," said Paul. "The bear hasn't seen us yet. You boys stay low and go to the tree. Climb quickly and quietly. I'll stay here. After you get up the tree, I'll be coming right behind you."

Jim and Aaron bent down and slowly crept toward the tree.

Following Aaron, Jim whispered, "Stay down and move *fast!*"

Jim's heart was beating hard. He could hardly breathe. In a few seconds, the boys reached the tree.

Jim stood on a flat rock under the tree. He gave his brother a boost, and Aaron went up the tree without a sound. He climbed high among the branches.

Then Jim pulled himself up. He climbed about 10 feet above the ground and stood on a slim branch. Pushing some pine needles aside, he looked over at the bear. It was digging up plants and eating the roots.

Jim noticed that the animal had a

hump on its back. Its ears were small, and it had a silver ruff around its neck. *Oh, no! It was a grizzly!*

CHAPTER 8

Grizzly Attack

Jim could see his father working his way toward the tree. He was walking backward very quietly. *He'll reach the tree safely—the bear will never know he's there,* Jim thought to himself.

Then suddenly, the branch under Jim's feet snapped!

As Jim started to slip, his hands went out and he grabbed another branch that stopped his fall. Hanging on with all his strength, Jim slowly pulled himself up to a stronger branch. Then he looked around at the bear.

The huge grizzly had spun around and started to charge Paul! Some 1,000 pounds of fury was bearing down fast! Jim could see the bear's flashing teeth and hear it make a deep rumbling growl.

As Paul scrambled backward toward the tree, he tripped over a rock and dropped the spray can. The charging bear was less than 40 feet away. Jim *had* to help! He leaped out of the tree, grabbed the pepper spray, and aimed it at the bear. Then he pushed the trigger.

A stream of pepper spray hit the bear in the face. Its eyes blinded and stinging from the blast, the giant grizzly turned and ran toward the lake.

But the wind had blown some of the spray back at Paul and Jim! Both of them started to cough and gag. Tears streamed down their cheeks.

Aaron slid down the tree and led his father and brother to the stream.

"The bear's gone," he said. "Wash that stuff out of your eyes."

Both Paul and his son splashed their faces with cool water. About 20 minutes later, they started to feel better. Their stinging eyes were still bright red, but at least they were now able to see again.

Jim looked at his father and said, "Boy, that stuff really works."

"Good thing it does, or we might not be here right now," Paul answered.

They quickly made their way along the stream back to camp. Their nerves were on edge. Everywhere the boys looked they thought they saw a bear.

That was more excitement than I wanted, Jim thought to himself. He was relieved when they reached camp. Everything looked familiar and safe.

For a while, the three Barclays sat by the lake. Then the boys decided it was time to stop imagining bears. Instead, they went looking for the weasel.

"If you whistle, the weasel will pop out of the willows," Jim said.

He gave a short whistle, and sure enough, up popped the little weasel. He stared at the boys with his beady black eyes.

"Come and get me if you can," he

seemed to say. Then he disappeared into the willows by the spring.

Now it was time to start thinking about dinner. Jim made some soup and rice while Paul fried the trout on the propane stove. Both boys agreed that their father was right—the trout was so delicious it melted in their mouths!

After dinner, the boys helped clean up the camp. They didn't want any food around to attract another bear.

Darkness fell on the camp. Since there was no moon, the boys had to use their flashlights. They pulled their mats and sleeping bags out of the tent, laid back, and looked up at the stars.

This has been quite a day! they all thought to themselves.

CHAPTER 9

The Woods Are Closed

The head of the State Forestry Service had an appointment at the state office building in Helena. He was waiting for the governor to arrive. Peter Kent had been with the Forestry Service for 18 years. Just two years earlier, he'd been promoted to manage the department. At last the governor came in.

"Good morning, sir," Peter said. "I wonder if I could have 10 minutes of your time?"

"Sure thing, Peter," the governor said. "What's on your mind?"

"Governor," he said, "we have severe drought conditions all over the state.

Forest fire danger is extremely high. I'd like your permission to temporarily close the forests to all hiking, fishing, camping—just about everything."

The governor frowned.

"Is it really that bad?" he asked.

"Yes, sir, it is. In my 18 years in the department, I've never seen it this dry."

"Will closing the woods ensure that we won't have a fire, Peter?"

"No, sir, it won't do that. But it will reduce the chances of human error. Most importantly, it may keep some people from getting hurt. Of course, if the forces of nature start a fire—well, we can't do much about that."

Permission was granted. That afternoon, all the woods of Montana were closed to outdoor activities. But the Barclays, already 12 miles deep in the mountains, were unaware of this.

That morning over breakfast, Paul had suggested leaving Lodge Pole Lake.

"Look at the map, boys. There's a

remote mountain stream about seven miles east of here," he said. "I'll bet those trout have never seen a fly. If we hike through the woods, we can be there by late afternoon. The fishing should be great. What do you say, guys?"

Jim was the first to answer. "Okay, Dad—as long as that can of pepper spray isn't empty."

They packed their gear and were on their way by 9 o'clock. Following their map and compass, they reached the stream at about 3 o'clock in the afternoon. They set up a campsite and quickly got out their fishing gear.

Since the stream was small, they thought it best to fish in different spots.

Remembering yesterday's encounter with the grizzly, Aaron said, "But let's not get *too* far apart. I don't want to be far from that pepper spray."

As they fished the peaceful stream, the Barclays had no idea of what had happened earlier that day. A bolt of heat lightning had hit a lodge pole pine just four miles east of the stream. The tinder-dry tree had immediately caught fire.

The wind was blowing east to west, and soon the growing fire was moving west, too. By the time the fire was a mile from the stream, it was steadily burning a wide path through the forest.

Paul and the boys had just started to fish when Aaron shouted, "Look! There are two deer crossing the stream."

Paul and Jim glanced up just in time to see the bounding deer.

A minute later Jim said, "And look over there—it's a fox!"

At the same moment, Paul heard a crashing noise behind him. He turned in time to see a huge bull moose and three females crossing the stream just 75 yards below them. *What's going on?* he wondered. *Why are we seeing so many animals all of a sudden?*

Then Aaron said, "Listen! What's that noise?"

They all stood perfectly still. Off in the distance, Paul and Jim could now hear the strange sound from off in the distance. But none of the Barclays could identify what it was.

"I think I smell smoke," Jim said. Then, two more animals ran past them.

All of a sudden it hit Paul. All the animals running, the strange noises, the smoke—*it was a fire!*

"We have to get out of here!" Paul shouted. "That fire is moving toward us. That's why all the animals are running."

Led by their father, the two boys scrambled back to the campsite. They packed up their camping equipment as quickly as they could.

By now the smell of smoke was strong, and the sky was darkening. The thick black smoke from the fire was actually blocking the sun.

Aaron turned toward the stream and yelled, "*Look*, Dad! The fire is almost here!"

Paul stared in horror at the wall of flames. As far as he could see in both directions, there was nothing but fire. Just 50 yards below them the fire had already crossed the stream!

Now, heavy smoke filled the air, and breathing was difficult. And the roaring sound of the fire made it hard for the Barclays to hear each other's voices.

Paul turned and yelled at his sons. "Forget about the gear! Leave everything! *We have to make it back to the lake!"*

CHAPTER 10

Escaping the Fire

"Listen up, boys! This fire is moving fast, so we're going to have to move even faster," Paul cried out.

Leaving everything behind them, the frightened campers started running west toward the lake.

The air temperature was heating up! Sparks were landing all around them. And everywhere the sparks landed, flames sprouted up. Looking off to his right, Jim saw a wall of burning trees.

"Dad," he said in a choking voice. "Dad, the fire is gaining on us."

"Keep moving, son. We just have to find openings in the flames."

Suddenly, a blazing lodge pole pine came crashing down to the forest floor. It fell just 20 yards in front of the Barclays!

"Let's try to jump the trunk, guys!" Paul yelled. "Going around it will waste too much time."

Jim cleared the tree easily, and so did Paul. But Aaron stumbled and fell. The flames surrounded him as he lay on the ground. A few sparks fell on his clothing and started to smoke. *Oh, no!* he thought to himself. *Am I on fire?*

Jim had seen his brother fall. In an instant, he'd jumped back over the burning log. Now he pulled his brother to his feet.

Paul screamed, *"This way, Jim!"*

Jim led Aaron back to the log and lifted him over it. Paul reached out and caught Aaron on the other side. "Are you okay, son?" he asked worriedly.

"Yeah—I just tripped."

Now Jim jumped back across the log. He helped Paul pat down his little brother's smoking clothes.

"You must be pretty hot stuff,

Aaron—you're *smoking*," Jim teased.

"Only you could make jokes at a time like this," Aaron groaned.

By now, all three Barclays were struggling to breathe. To filter out the smoke, they covered their noses and mouths with their wadded up shirts.

Paul figured they'd gone about three miles—not even halfway to the lake yet. *But, at least we seem to be keeping up with the fire,* he thought to himself. *We may not be gaining on it, but I don't think it's gaining on us, either.*

It was so dark now that Paul had difficulty reading his compass. *We've got to keep heading west,* he thought. *If we go the wrong way and miss the lake— No, I don't want to even think about that!*

The nearest forest ranger station had already reported the fire. Water-carrying helicopters were on their way to the area. Teams of special firefighters were also being organized to put out the raging forest fire.

If this fire couldn't be stopped, it would destroy thousands of acres of woodland. The state would do anything it could to stop the blaze.

Paul figured that now they couldn't be more than two miles from Lodge Pole Lake. He turned to his sons.

"Not too much farther to the lake, guys. We can make it," he said.

Their progress had been slowed down, however. Jim was now helping Aaron to keep up. When he got too tired, Paul would take over.

"This wouldn't be quite so hard for me if the air was easier to breathe," Aaron said between coughs.

"I know, son. The smoke is awful."

The little group was moving slower and slower. They were getting tired. And the intense heat and smoke were having an effect. Aaron was struggling even harder to keep up. At every step, the flames were still licking at their heels. *We've got to reach the lake soon*, Paul thought.

Jim was leading the way now. He was about 10 yards ahead of his father and brother. After going over a little rise, he turned and yelled, "Dad—I think I see the lake!"

Paul and Aaron made it over the rise. Jim was right. There was Lodge Pole Lake about 200 yards ahead!

"We made it, guys!" Paul shouted.

Hopeful now, they all broke into a desperate run for the lake.

At the water's edge, they pushed some fallen logs into the water. Hanging on for their lives, they started paddling for the middle of the lake.

The cool water felt wonderful. After a few minutes, all three looked back at the fire. It had reached the water's edge and was starting to move around the lake. They stared at the raging blaze in silence. They'd made it to safety by no more than three or four minutes!

Paul finally spoke. "Whew! That's cutting things a little close," he said.

Both boys smiled.

"It sure is," Jim said. "I can't believe I was worried that this trip might be boring."

CHAPTER 11

Back at the Motel

For several hours, the Barclays floated on their logs in the lake. Soot and smoke hung in the air, making a dirty gray film on the water. And now it was also very dark. Paul glanced at his watch. It was midnight.

"We can't try to walk out of here in the dark," Paul said. "We'll have to spend the night on the edge of the lake. Heck— it'll be light out in six hours. We can handle that, can't we, guys?"

The floating logs had carried them several miles past the fire. As they sat on the edge of the lake, Aaron said, "Gee, I hope all the animals made it out okay."

"There's a good chance that most of them did, Aaron," Paul said. "They have a natural instinct for escaping a fire."

For a while, they were quiet. Each of them was thinking about everything that had happened.

Finally, Jim spoke. "You know, Dad— trips with you are never boring."

"I guess you're right, Jimbo. We've had some awfully exciting adventures, haven't we, boys?"

"Yeah—in some cases, *too* exciting," Aaron piped up.

"I want both of you to know that I'm proud of how you handled yourselves," Paul said. "Dealing with the bear and the fire took real courage."

Jim and Aaron grinned at their father.

"Thanks, Dad," they said together.

At 6:15 the next morning, it was light enough to see the trail. Paul and the boys started back.

Since most of the walking was downhill, it was easier. Also, they had no camping gear to carry. Everything had been lost in the fire. Paul figured it would take them about four hours to get back to Marble Fork. And sure enough, they reached their car at 11 o'clock.

"Let's go down to Elmer's and spend the night there," Paul suggested. "A hot shower, a good meal, and a soft bed will feel just great."

"Fine with us," Jim said.

"Dad," Aaron asked, "don't you think we should stop somewhere and buy some clothes?"

Paul glanced at his two sons. They looked liked hobos! Their clothes were dirty and torn. Their faces were smudged with black soot. In several places, their shirts and pants were riddled with burn holes. He started to laugh.

"What's so funny, Dad?" Jim asked.

"You boys don't know how bad you look," Paul said.

"Well, Dad, *you* don't look so great yourself! Do you know your eyebrows are singed?" Aaron said as he pointed at his father's face.

Now all three of them were laughing.

"You're right, Aaron. Before we go to Elmer's, we'll get some new clothes. Heck, looking like this, they probably wouldn't let us in the motel anyway."

That evening the Barclays walked into Elmer's dining room. Helen greeted them and showed them to a table.

"Helen—this time we have a story for *you*," Paul said. "We were caught in that forest fire up near Lodge Pole Lake."

"No kidding!" she gasped.

"Yeah," Jim jumped in. "We ran ahead of that fire for six or seven miles."

"Wow!" she said. "That's exciting."

"And," Aaron added, "we got attacked by a grizzly bear."

"Holy smokes! After what you guys have been through, Elmer may give you a free dinner tonight—if you'll tell him your story, that is."

Paul chuckled. "To quote one of your regular customers, 'I'd tell my story to the devil for a free dinner.'"

Helen looked puzzled, but Jim and Aaron roared with laughter. They were both hoping Zeb Parker would walk in—but he didn't.

The next day they drove back to the Bozeman airport for the flight home.

After they boarded the plane, Aaron turned to his father and said, "You know what, Dad? Mom's never going to believe what happened this week."

"Oh, yes, she will," his father sighed. "I think she's getting used to it."

COMPREHENSION QUESTIONS

Remembering Details

1. Which bear is bigger—a black bear or a grizzly?

2. What kind of legal permits did the Barclays have to buy?

3. Why can't brown bears climb trees?

4. At Lodge Pole Lake, what animals howled at night?

5. What started the forest fire?

6. What smell in the air alerted the Barclays to danger?

7. What did the Barclays have to buy before their last dinner at Elmer's?

Who and Where?

1. What was the destination (city and state) of the Barclays' flight?

2. Who explained the difference between black bears and grizzlies to the Barclays?

3. Who said that trout always bite better in the morning than at night?

4. What nickname does Paul sometimes use for his son, Jim?

5. Which two Barclays got hit with pepper spray?

6. Who fell while trying to jump over a burning tree trunk?

7. Who lost part of his leg when he was attacked by a grizzly bear?

8. At what lake did the Barclays pitch their first campsite?